GÉNÃRÕ

LOST IN THE SWAMP

A.J.N. GALLAGHER

LOST IN THE SWAMP

A.J.N. Gallagher

First Edition: 2021-05-17 v1.2

Second Edition: 2024-04-4 v1.3

ISBN-13: 978-0-473-57598-4 (EPUB)
ISBN-13: 978-0-473-57599-1 (KINDLE)
ISBN-13: 978-0-473-58595-2 (Softcover print-on-demand)
ISBN-13: 978-0-473-66071-0 (Hardback POD)

Artwork by Elana Bai

Dedication

To My Dad

Lost in the swamp

On a forgotten world, a shadow of what it once was, Taren Fairwater rode his single-engine Waterhog through the heart of the vast swamp. His ride left a serpentine wake as it weaved rhythmically between the tall, smooth-sided badong trees that rose from the water's eerie depths. The sound of the Waterhog's throaty engine drowned out the torrential rain on the canopy above. When he left early that morning from his home outside the sleepy swamp-side village of Lorn, there wasn't a cloud in the sky, the first rays of sunlight promising the perfect day for a test run.

He had found it while out fishing for trill with his adoptive father, Arlorn. A flash storm the previous day had shifted a debris cluster to reveal the rusty remains of the pre-Fall relic.

From then on, it occupied his every waking moment, dulling the traumatic events at the orphanage in Gwell, events that brought him into Arlorn's care and to his little stilt house on the edge of Lorn.

Taren scoured every backyard scraper and backwash hoarder for parts to rebuild the Waterhog. And when those ran dry, he adapted parts from other pre-Fall relics, until after three years, his ride was ready for its first trial run.

The morning he left, he promised Arlorn he wouldn't travel too far into the swamp. He waved excitedly to Arlorn standing on the little wharf attached to the front of his house. Arlorn's eyebrows furrowed in a look Taren had grown accustomed to. The morning light accentuated the grey flecks that highlighted his hair. A grey that Taren swore wasn't there when he first came into Arlorn's care.

Taren headed into the shallow waters around Lorn. But it wasn't long until the wake from his Waterhog acquired a torrent of angry oaths from pole-boat fishermen heading out to their hunting grounds for the day. Taren forced his way out beyond the remains of the great wall that marked the watery border of Lorn. He turned the Waterhog into the wilds of the great swamp.

Once out in the deeper waters, Taren soon forgot his promise to Arlorn. With the feeling of the powerful engine between his legs and the wind on his face, he soon found himself deep in the western swamp. A place where the trees grew tall and unchecked. A place where even the bravest fishermen feared to go; and the few that would return came back wide-eyed and rambling about monstrous creatures and ghosts that haunted their every step.

Taren passed long-necked water breathers who paused from feeding on the low-reaching leech ferns and ghost lichens that hung from the canopy. He watched as they continued dozily chewing their cud until they disappeared from sight.

Menacing shapes appeared beneath the surface, their wakes bulging as they trailed behind. But the followers soon lost interest when they found they were no match for the Waterhog's speed. Taren toyed with them, allowing them to get close then speeding away, enjoying the power the Waterhog brought him. So engrossed was Taren with his game, he was unaware of a shadow lurking in the waters ahead.

By the time Taren saw the creature, it was too late. The water erupted around him as he reached the centre, engulfing him in a shower of liquid before sucking him down into the maelstrom of the creature's cavernous mouth. His ride circled in the swirling water as it drained to whatever lay beneath the gurgling throat.

He opened the throttle and leaned the Waterhog against the walls of its slimy mouth, trying to gain momentum as he spiralled towards the narrowing opening. Teeth appeared near the top, curving inwards to cut off his escape. Taren opened the throttle.

The Waterhog shuddered as it broke through the teeth and cleared the mouth. A fragment hit the dash, then narrowly missed Taren's face. The Waterhog landed with a splash into the waters nearby, submerging beneath the surface only to resurface a moment later as the rear track caught water. The creature let out a gargled moan as it submerged beneath the surface once more until only the shadow remained. There it would continue its vigil, patiently waiting for its next victim to come within reach.

Taren opened his eyes and gasped from the cold of the water. His body drenched, he could feel the water draining down his back and into his boots. His eyes grew even wider as he stared at the ten-tentacled water leech caught on the Waterhog's headlamp. The leech's one big eye glared at Taren, unamused at being removed from its watery environment. They stared at each other for a moment, causing Taren to miss the submerged log up ahead. The front ski hit the log, lifting the Waterhog out of the water. The leech lost its grip and landed on Taren's face. He struggled to breathe as the leech wrapped its tentacles around his head, muffling his panicked scream as they stared eye to eye.

Taren felt the leech's proboscis reaching inside his mouth, so he did the only thing he could. He bit down, hard. The leech let go; all his tentacles hung limp. Taren swung his head to the side to dislodge it, spitting out the foul taste of its proboscis. The leach landed with a 'plop' in the water then swam as fast as its ten tentacles could take it to the safety of the blackened depths.

Time for home, thought Taren as he sped away, wishing he had something to wash away the leach's foul taste. He reached for the homing compass on the handlebars, but fear gripped him when he saw the cracked glass and the needle spinning uncontrollably. He looked frantically to the sun for direction, but the sky was darkening behind an approaching storm. Before long, he was straining to see through the torrential rain and greying trees. The sounds of deadfall branches crashed around him as night closed in.

He rode his Waterhog close to the bigger trees, hoping the root system beneath the surface would keep the larger predators at bay. Skimming hurriedly from one tree to the next, he desperately looked for somewhere safe for the night. All the while, Arlorn's words played over and over in his mind.

"Always remember, time will be your friend in the morning but your worst enemy in the afternoon. Return to landfall before the sun's shadow stretches to the east. For the mooring behind is surer than the hope of the mooring imagined in front of you."

As the last rays of light faded into gloom, Taren could hear creatures swimming around him. Tears welled up in his eyes. He knew he wouldn't survive the night. He sighed, wiped stinging tears from his eyes, and turned off the engine. If this was going to be the end, he didn't want to see it coming. He hoped it would be quick.

Something caught Taren's attention. A single ray of light had pierced the canopy, illuminating a solitary badong tree in the waters ahead. There was a hole at the base, partially obscured with vines and leech ferns swaying in the storm. A hollow that may be large enough to accommodate him and his Waterhog for the night.

He kick-started the Waterhog to life and accelerated towards the opening. But as he got closer, he wondered what else could be sheltering in there from the storm.

He only had one weapon at his disposal. Well, more for defense. Something he cobbled together himself and what Arlorn insisted he add before embarking on any journey into the swamp. He was pretty proud of it if he said so himself.

He flicked a button on the handlebars, and a barrel from

the compressed air cannon slid forward on the frame below the fuel tank. Coming within range of the tree, he pressed a button, and a 'whompf' issued as it propelled a gas canister into the opening. Smoke billowed from the trunk as Taren rode past it. An array of creepies and white-eyed, winged night suckers retreated from the acrid fumes.

Taren leaned his Waterhog into a wide arc, slowly circling back through the surrounding trees as he waited for the smoke to disperse. Once the smoke subsided, he lined himself up for the trunk, unaware of the water swelling behind him.

A grey lump emerged from the swell. A toothless mouth appeared, towering above Taren. The bottom jaw slipped silently underneath while excess water vented from gills on its side and propelled it forward. As it was about to clamp shut, the creature halted, some invisible force stopping it in its tracks. It recoiled in pain, disappearing under a broil of frothing water.

Taren looked behind but only saw the receding water. The hairs on the back of his neck stood on end. He opened the throttle and climbed further up his seat and away from whatever it was.

He bridged the gap to the tree but realised he was going too fast. He slammed the Waterhog into reverse, the force almost throwing him over the handlebars as he entered the trunk. The Waterhog stopped inches from the opposite wall. Having pushed a wave of water in front of him, it now crashed over Taren before flooding out of the opening.

Taren sat motionless, staring wide-eyed at the wall in front of him. After a moment, he let out a long sigh and shook the last of the drips from his sopping hair. He manoeuvred himself around to face the entrance, then pulled up the hood for his cloak and waited for the morning light.

He shivered as he listened to the rain and wind outside and wondered how he would ever find his way back without his compass. The only tools were at his workshop next to his nice warm bed.

My bed, he thought. What he wouldn't give to be nursing a steaming bowl of Arlorn's slugmutt root soup, a soup so thick you could stand a spoon up in it, with its fragrant flavours of trill and nutty swamp root. His stomach rumbled in agreement too, so he tried to think of something else.

He tried to remember Arlorn's teaching on 'right mind,' as he called it. He would scoff whenever Arlorn brought it up, but now he wished he'd paid more attention to the words. "Count your Undra," he would say. "Your attitude will always take you further than your circumstances ever could."

Those words always left Taren angry and confused him, even when Arlorn would take the time to explain. What made it worse was his smile. That annoying, knowing smile that made Taren even more frustrated. He would storm off in frustration until he had calmed enough to continue Arlorn's teachings.

Arlorn had a patience that seemed to permeate each facet of his life. Whether cleaning trill for market or attending to the most mundane task, Arlorn's patience would always shine through.

Taren laughed, his voice reverberating through the trunk. The absurdity of Arlorn's words playing over in his head, but then… in the darkness, something made sense, and for the first time, he finally realised what Arlorn meant.

"Count your blessings," said Taren quietly to himself. He looked around the trunk in the darkness and did just that. He reminded himself of how fortunate he was to have found somewhere to stay. And even though his compass was broken, Arlorn's other words came to mind: "Tomorrow is tomorrow's problem, and tomorrow will always take care of itself." Taren smiled, and as he did, a peace rose in his chest.

As the night drew on, Taren's eyes grew heavy, lulled by

melodic drips that fell within the walls, but as he sat in the dark, a sound caught his attention.

He pulled back his hood and listened closer.

There it was again, the sound of water dripping on metal.

Taren turned on the Waterhog's front light and glimpsed a shape within the folds of the matted vines near the opening. He edged closer and carefully eased the vines aside, revealing a rusty switchboard with levers on the front. Above each lever was a symbol. He had seen them in the books that Arlorn would force him to study, the books of the old language, the ones he was now thankful he had learned. Well… sort of. Enough to get a general idea. "Hmm," muttered Taren.

He studied them for a while, frustration growing on his face. Eventually, he gave up and, with a disgruntled huff, he pulled the first lever.

The sound of protesting machinery filled the trunk, and the water beneath the Waterhog broiled. A small wharf rose from the turbulent depths beside him. Aquatic life pulled from their underwater home slithered and scurried off the wharf, their milky eyes blind to the world around them and their feelers sensing for the dark once more. Taren excitedly pulled the next lever, and the sound of crunching metal filled the trunk once more as an imposing, heavy steel door burst through a veil of vines above the opening. The vines and roots snapped as the door lowered into place to seal the entrance.

"Well, that's impressive," said Taren and eagerly pulled the next lever.

A swishing sound filled the air as long, blade-like steps unfolded from the trunk wall. The steps circled up the inside of the trunk to the darkness above, each one illuminated by a small light at the base that came on as they locked into place with a solid 'thunk.'

A light appeared above the switchboard, buzzing dimly

and yellow with age, and Taren noticed a place for a fourth lever off to the side. The shaft was missing, and only a metal stub remained. He felt inside the stub with his fingers and could feel raised markings inside. He had seen similar mechanisms in the books Arlon had shown him. They were called key-levers and could only be operated by a lever that fitted into the markings inside. He looked around for the lever but to no avail. Whatever secret the lever held, he wouldn't be opening it without the handle. He might have better luck in the morning light, so he would try then, but for now, he had to see what lay at the top of the stairs.

Taren moored the Waterhog to the wharf and switched off the headlight, then tried the first step, tentatively feeling the weight under his feet. The step creaked but held his weight, so he made his way up the circling steps to the darkness above, testing each stair as he went.

As he reached the top, the last few steps turned abruptly inwards, disappearing into a short tunnel carved into the centre of the trunk. A heavy-set door lay at the end of the tunnel, illuminated by a buzzing nicotine-tinted light.

Taren stepped over the threshold, and without warning, the steps retracted behind him. The light at the base of each step winked out as they folded against the wall. All Taren could do was watch as the steps and lights spiralled away from him down the trunk until he was all alone in the darkness with only the dimly buzzing light above the door for company. He scoured the tunnel for a lever to bring back the steps but found none. With nowhere to go but forward, he looked to the door in front of him.

There were deep gouges in the wooden door. Taren ran his fingers in the groves. Whatever it was, it was powerful, the force from the claws even cutting into the iron nails.

He wondered how long ago this had been done, comforting himself that the answer was most likely a long, long time ago. He looked into the darkness behind him. "Most likely."

At that moment, Taren decided it would be more beneficial to be on the other side of the door. He looked for the latch but only found claw marks where the latch once sat. The metal around it was twisted and broken.

Taren smiled to himself. He wouldn't let the minor matter of a broken lock stand in his way. It had never stopped him in the past—to Arlorn's dismay.

He had promised Arlorn he would get rid of his Magna-key after the incident with Don Tanwai. But fortunately for Taren, he hadn't the heart to throw it away. *And in this case,* he thought, *technically I'm breaking into a...* He didn't actually know what he was breaking into, but since the latch was missing, it couldn't be classified as breaking in; more like assisting a repair.

Removing a fist-sized magnet from his shoulder satchel, Taren placed it over the remains of the latch, delicately moving it around while he felt the weight of the magnet pull against the metal within the door.

There was a click, and the door shuddered, releasing a puff of dust as it opened a fraction inwards.

"Never fails," said Taren with a smile, kissing the magnet and placing it back into his pouch.

He tried the door. His smile turned to a frown as the door refused to budge. He braced himself and, with a heave and a push, the door slowly opened inwards, protesting loudly on its ancient hinges. Taren's mouth hung open as he stared speechless around the room.

The door opened into the lower level of a circular tree-house. Green cushioned bench seats lined the wall, circling a large stone fireplace at its centre. A wide-rimmed flue covered the top of the fireplace, supported by hearty beams that circled the conical-shaped room. The chimney sported pulleys and cables up its length, allowing for it to be raised or lowered as needed.

Taren spotted an alcove beneath the stone fireplace stacked to the brim with firewood, and it wasn't long until he had a fire ablaze and was relaxing on the soft bench seats. He could feel the warmth permeating his wet clothes, the soft crackling and dancing flames lulling him to sleep as the rain and wind raged outside. His body was too exhausted to explore the rest of the house, and his mind was dreaming of slugmutt root soup.

The Nest

Taren woke the following day to feel the sun on his face. Wispy clouds passed overhead, joined by rising mist from the morning heat. The edges tossed and tussled like fraying silk, dancing in a fleeting embrace before dissolving into the morning sun. The smell of sun after the rain filled his nostrils; it reminded him of how a new day could bring the promise of a new beginning. Well, that's what Arlorn used to say.

Taren frowned and sat up, the last of his sleep vanishing from his mind as he stared at the roof, or the lack of it.

The roof was made of black, see-through mesh fabric kept taught by intricate fixtures along each beam. It covered the entire expanse except where the chimney breached. The top of the chimney was capped with a cone with vents in the side for the smoke.

The mesh stopped at the wooden walls, where pillars on the outside edge supported the beams that fanned out from the chimney. The circular shape of the house made each section look like a segment of an orange.

There was a set of stairs that divided the bench seats on the far side of the fireplace, so Taren made his way up to the main floor for a better look. The wall was low enough that he could see out above the roof, and to his delight, he found the house was nestled just above the canopy. He could see the snow-topped mountains to the west, where those who travelled never returned and where strange lights flickered on occasion. To the east lay the Escarpment Mountains that ran north to south, bordering the Midlands Valley and the Forbidden Desert that lay beyond it.

The swamp ran west to east, turning into a braided delta known as the Shārtūa Delta before emptying at the Eastern Sea. It divided the land and could only be traversed by a five-

11

day journey between Lorn on the south shore and Gwell on the north, but also by the two paddle boats that ferried goods between them.

A glint of light winked at Taren from the mountains. Taren knew that could only be one thing—the crystal cathedral from the Highland Temple glinting in the morning sun. He followed the mountain range south with his finger to where it abruptly stopped above the Shārtūa Delta that flowed out to the sea.

He smiled. "That means," said Taren to himself, "that Lorn would be about…" His finger stopped where Lorn would be. Now he knew the way home. All he just needed to set up a temporary Magna-compass on his handlebars, take a bearing as he left the treehouse, and he'd be home. Arlorn was right. Tomorrow had taken care of itself.

A rustle from the neighbouring trees woke Taren from his musing. A family of long-tailed weelix appeared from beneath the foliage to bask in the sun. The boisterous behaviour of the younger ones made Taren smile. Their escapades escalated till one of the younger ones bit one of the older one's tail. The resulting uproar forced the elder weelix to step in and bring them into line. Taren burst into laughter as the antics were repeated a few moments later.

The weelix stopped and sat up, their little black noses twitching while their lime-green eyes scoured for the source of the noise. Their hoots grew louder and more agitated as they searched for the unseen source. Taren didn't understand why they hadn't seen him. Spotting a small door leading out to a loading balcony, he went outside for a better look. As soon as Taren opened the door, the weelix disappeared beneath the foliage, whooping and howling as they went.

It wasn't until he looked back at the roof from the outside that he understood why they hadn't seen him. The mesh was like a one-way mirror, obscuring those inside from the outside world. Taren had never seen anything like it. He reached out and touched the mesh.

A blue spark ripped up his arm, and he recoiled in pain; the weelix receded further into the trees from all the commotion.

"All right. Don't touch the roof."

As he massaged some feeling back into his fingers, a large beetle-fly landed on the mesh. It immediately erupted into blue goo with a sickening crack. The remains of its wings fluttering like feathers to the waters beneath.

"Hmm," Taren mused as he watched the wings flutter from sight. "That would've been most helpful to see a few seconds ago."

Taren remembered stories of houses before the Fall, technology that turned light into energy. 'Electramesh' they called it. But none survived. Most were stripped or destroyed in the first few years, and the people who were left to fend for themselves fought over resources. Apparently, one had survived. It made sense, though, way out here where no one could find it.

He pondered the house as he stared out over the loading bay balcony to the waters beneath. Fish and shadowy shapes patrolled the swamp, circling the trunk while predatory insects left rings as they touched the surface, searching for water-boatmen. But as he watched, he noticed the aquatic life circled out near the surrounding tree-line, away from the trunk, as if an invisible force kept them away.

The longer he looked, the more perplexed he became. The fish followed a regimented line in the water, but as far as he could tell, there was nothing physically stopping them from getting closer. And if there were, it would have stopped him last night. With nothing obvious outside, Taren thought he would look elsewhere for the answer, so he went inside for a look.

Just inside the doorway, Taren found a panel like the one at the base of the trunk. He pulled the lever and listened, but heard nothing, so he returned to the balcony. To his surprise, the marine life leisurely circling the trunk now swam to the base of the tree and began to feed on the waterline weeds and trunk slugs that were previously out of reach.

With the mystery solved, Taren returned inside and reset the lever. The sounds of frenzied splashing broke the relative silence of the swamp. Taren returned to the balcony in time to see the water seething in a broiling mess. Marine life swam to their original position near the tree line then continued with their circling once more. Some of the larger shapes eyed Taren warily as they circled.

Taren still didn't understand why the marine life avoided the trunk, so he tried the lever a few more times, returning to the balcony each attempt in hopes of a glimpse of this invisible force. After several attempts, he saw a shimmer pulse out through the water from the trunk.

He laid his hand on the trunk and felt the faintest tremor; he closed his eyes and placed his ear to the surface. There was a sound like a musical note, a discordant note, but a note nonetheless. *How clever, using sound to keep marine life away,* thought Taren.

Taren wondered what other secrets this place held; this place nestled amongst the canopy like a nest.

A nest.

"That's it!" That's what he would call it—the Nest.

That was, of course, if no one else had a claim to it. The Nest seemed relatively in order, and—apart from the claw marks on the stairwell door—there was no other damage. The only thing that didn't look right was at the far side of the room, where a tree trunk-framed bed held a large lump beneath animal skin covers.

Taren approached with some hesitancy. The outline of a

decayed body stained the skins; a skull above the sheets etched a halo of decay into the pillow. Wisps of long red hair clung to the skull while a weaved beard hung close to the chin. The head, resting in Taren's direction, haunted him as if it were asking a question.

Under the remains of a skeletal hand lay an open, leather-bound journal with an insignia embossed in silver and gold at the top of the page. The last entry had been scrawled by a grey flutter-flight quill that still lay clasped between the long, white finger bones.

Curious about the writing, Taren carefully slipped the journal out from beneath the hand, but before it released, it tore apart.

"Oops...!" Taren looked at the occupant, expecting a rebuke. When none came forth, he relaxed and laughed at the absurdity of his thoughts.

His smile faded as the skull turned to face him, resettling after he disturbed the body.

"Sorry." Taren hung his head, feeling he should show more respect.

There was a bedside cabinet nearby, so he gently laid the journal on top, trying to piece it together as best he could, all the while giving the occupant an apologetic smile.

The skull slumped forward, causing Taren to tear the journal even more. Again, he tried to piece it together, but the more he tried, the worse it got. Parts of the journal crumbled like fire-burned tissue, fluttering gently to the floor while Taren apologised profusely at the skull, which stared empty-eyed at him. Finally, he gave up, only the last entry remaining intact amongst the bed of fragments.

"Well, that didn't go as I expected." His face flushed with embarrassment, and he tried to feign a smile.

He looked at the page in front of him, too scared to look at the skull in case it moved again. He recognised the words from the old language; a language Arlorn had forced him to learn as part of his homeschooling. Arlorn always swore that one day it could save his life.

Taren would always roll his eyes and begrudgingly learn the words. Not that they weren't easy to understand. He had a knack for languages. It's just he would rather work on his Waterhog or hunt the scrapyards for parts. But at this moment in time, he was grateful for Arlorn's schooling.

Taren pawed over each word, mouthing each symbol and phrase until the words made sense in his mind. He cleared his throat and spoke the words out loud, as Arlorn always taught him to do.

Welcome

It is with great sadness that I will be unable to greet you in person, for my time is near.

The beast that once tormented these waters has been stayed by my own hand. But sadly, this has come at great cost. For even now, I feel the life that once flowed through these veins souring from the monster's poisoned claws.

Do not be saddened at my passing, for I will now join those who have gone before, happy in the knowledge that you, as my successor, will continue the good work left to us.

My last petition is that I am buried in accordance with our order. For though my soul will rise to receive its reward, this body will return to the dust from whence it came.

On the bookshelf, you will find the book Lavie De Alosa Terranaie, and within its pages, you will find the map to my final resting place.

As my replacement, I relinquish to you all that is within these walls. In particular, the books penned by my own hand and those left behind from others before. They are yours now; may they serve you well, and may you find enlightenment in this world and in the one to come.

Finally, I pass on to you the token of our commitment, my scep-tre. Carry it and the symbol it represents with honour as you con-tinue the good work.

Your Beloved Servant

Fēómin Lõnstāē.

3rd of Anctari. 2431

There was a postscript at the bottom of the page. The words trailed off into a strange symbol, Taren only making out one phrase: *What is above is also below.*

Taren looked at the date again. "You've been here for a long time. Well before the Fall."

He felt a sense of sadness for Fēómin Lõnstāē. Left alone all this time, waiting for someone who would never come to ful-fil his last wish, the Fall had seen to that. In some ways, Fēómin was lucky. He never saw what happened to this world when the Off-worlders arrived. The three-day war leading to the destruction of the Everlight city. The fact that the Elders destroyed the city rather than allow whatever they were protecting inside to fall into the Off-worlders' hands. But that was only a rumour, and after a thousand years, no one knew for sure. All anyone knew was the fallout from the Everlight city's destruction—a Null Field that continues to permeate the planet, dampening all high energy technology that once dominated it. Essentially, cutting the planet off from the stars. *Fēómin is lucky not to see how far it has fallen*, thought Taren.

He wasn't much given to moments of compassion, but as he looked at Fēómin's remains and thought of how long he had lain there, something tugged at his conscience. The longer he looked, the stronger the tugging became.

"Alright," sighed Taren as he threw his arms in the air. "I'll bury you."

He was about to look for the bookshelf with the map when

he noticed a leather belt hanging from the bedpost. A scabbard sewn along the middle contained a wooden handle bearing the same silver and gold insignia as the journal.

He carefully removed it and held it up to the light, turning it over in his hand. As he did so, a grotesque bug appeared on the end. Instinctively he gave it a flick. The handle shook violently and a wide, flat blade as long as Taren's forearm unfolded from it, the tip sporting a small backward hook along the flat edge.

"Wow!" Taren held it up to the light. "A Bushblade. I never thought I'd ever see one of these."

He gave the handle another flick, and the Bushblade folded neatly into itself. Taren spent the next few minutes flicking the handle, folding and unfolding the weapon, and feeling the weight in his hands before re-sheathing it. He looked at Fēómin's remains for a moment, then, with a smile and a nod, he donned the belt.

"Of course, I'll look after it for you. And if your replacement ever arrives, I'll be sure to pass it on to them. Think of it as safekeeping 'til then, and…" he smiled "…payment for fulfilling your last wish."

He found the book *Lavie De Alosa Terranaie* wedged between two towering leather-backed volumes. The books had the author's names torn off, with only the first and last letters T…….. n visible on each spine. The map was hidden within.

Taren gently bundled up Fēómin's remains in the bed coverings and tied the ends up into loops to form a backpack. Next, he found a fold-away spade amongst the tools in the Nest. Then, he headed to the stairwell.

It wasn't until he got to the doorway that he remembered the stairs had folded away after his ascent. While he wondered how he would get down, he noticed a lever beside the door. He pulled the lever, and the sounds of steps unfolding echoed up the stairwell.

"Amazing." Taren headed down the stairs and out into the swamp.

The Cave

He followed the map through the waterways, the marked trees showing him the way. He was surprised the trees were still there after all this time, but then again, no one came this far into the swamp. The trees were so imposing that even damaged and minus some branches, they were undeniably the right trees. And, of course, he did have the map.

It wasn't long until he came to an island shaped like a giant slug protruding from the water. The top was covered with a carpet of moss and ferns that draped down its steep sides into the water like unkempt hair. The back end trailed off into the water while the front opened like a gaping mouth, obscured by vines and clinger ferns that partially covered the opening. Steps led up to the mouth of the cave, adorned with mooring posts at the water's edge.

He had heard tell of similar caves scattered throughout the planet, made from the same black stone that formed the walls of Gwell and other pre-Fall civilisations now inhabited by the current races. Rumours were, the caves ran on for miles, and no one ever found the end to them. It was also rumoured that those that ventured too far in were never heard of again.

Taren moored the Waterhog and cautiously climbed the steps, then bit his lip as he stared into the darkness within. The list of reasons for not entering grew as his imagination toyed with the horrors he might find inside. A breath of wind patted a fern frond aside, the penetrating sunlight revealing a tanic dung-tar lantern on the cave wall just inside.

"Hmm," said Taren. "Oh well, I've come this far." He took a deep breath of courage and stepped over the threshold, ignoring a breath of chilling air that washed over him as if the cave had sighed.

He pulled the lantern from its hold and lit it with his flint light. The oily smell of tanic beetle tar made him cough. Black smoke blistered off the crusty shell as it burnt away, the dung within erupting into blue flame and illuminating Taren in a soft hue.

More lanterns lined the wall, so Taren lit each one and followed the steps into the bowels of the cave. His footsteps echoed around the walls as he went, accompanied by melodic drips that plopped in time with his steps and a trickle of water that gargled down the middle of the cave. He continued on for some time, wondering how deep this cave was. He guessed he must be well below the watery bottom of the swamp, and the thought of all that water just outside the cave walls made him nervous, never having learned how to swim.

The cave levelled off, but at the same time, the trail of lanterns abruptly stopped. Taren felt rather uneasy with only his solitary lantern for comfort. He hoped the burial ground wasn't too far ahead and continued, occasionally looking back to the lights that slowly faded from sight.

He came to a shallow lake filled with pooling water, his lantern light unable to see the other side. He picked up a handful of stones and threw them into the water, hearing the deep 'bloop' of each stone echo around the cavern.

"Well. I guess that's it," he said with some relief. "Too deep to cross."

He looked for somewhere nearby to bury Fēómin's remains but tripped over a rock protruding from the ground. He landed face down in the mud and grazed his knee, the blue light of his lantern extinguished with a hiss on the wet cavern floor, casting Taren into utter darkness.

Fumbling around, he frantically felt for the lantern but only found its sodden remains. He nursed his throbbing knee, his pain turning to anger, and berated himself for agreeing to bury Fēómin.

His eyes adjusted to the darkness and could just make out

the water's edge. He picked up Fēómin's remains and walked to the edge, steeling himself as he prepared to throw them in. Pausing, he lowered the remains. That was no way to care for the dead. And he had promised.

He stared out into the mirror black waters. The pain in his knee began to subside with his anger, and somehow, he knew he had made the right decision. But still, he had nowhere to bury Fēómin, let alone see his way back.

While he postulated, stars began to appear on the water's surface. The cave became brighter as more of them appeared until the cave was bathed in a soft, blue-white hue. He looked up and saw the stars were actually suspended from the ceiling.

"Stella grubs!" said Taren. "I wish Arlorn was here. He will never believe me."

More appeared on the walls, like thousands of tiny candles, until Taren was drenched in light. The whole cave, including the pond, except...

Taren frowned. A section three feet wide along the middle of the cavern ceiling was void of the stella grubs. The same image reflected on the water's surface. Taren threw a stone into the watery void. It bounced off the water's surface with a high-pitched 'click' and disappeared with a resounding 'bloop' into the starlit depths beside it.

This time Taren cast a stone along the darkened section. The stone skipped and bounced along the water before disappearing with a 'bloop' into the stella grub-lit depths. Taren prodded the water with his fold-away spade. The spade barely broke the surface before contacting solid ground beneath.

"A water bridge," said Taren with a smile, and he stepped onto it to make his way across the darkened section of the lake. His boots slapped on the shallow surface as he watched for any movement on the starlit black water on either side.

On the opposite shore was a graveyard that rose gently

from the starlit ground. An array of looming, ancient head-stones looked down at him as he walked between them. Some were in the shape of armoured men, their faces hidden beneath helmets, weapons at the ready, while others were winged apparitions with stern faces who gazed menacingly at him. Whoever this order was, thought Taren, they had been there for a very long time.

Taren looked for a place to bury Fēómin, but seeing nowhere suitable, he continued until he came to the end of the graves where he found an open grave with the soil mounded beside it. Taren felt his blood run cold as a chill swept through him and stared in silence at the gravestone in front of him. The words were written in the old tongue.

Fēómin Lõnstāē,
Watcher of the Western Tower
Keeper of the way.
May his passing
lead others to the light
and to those
that will follow after him

Taren felt pity for Fēómin. He had no idea that he was the last or the events that transpired after his death. There would be no one to carry on with… with… Well, whatever their order was doing out here.

He carefully lowered Fēómin's remains into the grave and covered them over with the dirt. "I'll say one thing about your order," said Taren as he shovelled the last spadeful onto the grave. "You certainly plan ahead."

With Fēómin's remains safely in the ground, Taren said a short prayer, remembering the words Arlorn would use for times like this. He spent a few moments looking out past the graveyard. There were no stella grubs out there, making it feel like the cave went on forever, shrouded in darkness and the secrets it held. Anything could be watching him, and for all he knew, something was. In fact, he had felt that for a while.

He noticed it was getting darker and looked up to see the Stella grubs on the edge of the darkness begin to wink out. *Time to leave*, thought Taren, as the darkness inched towards him. He briskly made his way back through the graveyard and onto the waterbridge, suppressing the urge to run, his feet slapping in the shallow water as he crossed the bridge.

Not Alone

Halfway across the waterbridge, Taren stopped and looked down at his feet. The hairs on the back of his neck prickled as the sounds of slapping coming up from behind continued without him. A creature sauntered out from the shadow behind him, its muscular, stony scaled form level with Taren's midriff. Green eyes glinted in the stella grub light as a guttural growl emanated from a mouth lined with large black teeth.

Beneath its legs, smaller pairs of green eyes appeared, like a multi-eyed spider. Taren shuddered, he hated spiders, but his fear turned to relief as four cubs appeared from beneath her legs and squealed with a high-pitched growl at him. Taren chuckled at the adorable quartet, but his levity faded as the quartet turned into a quintet with the addition of the mother's protective growl.

A long, powerful tail curled around the cubs, corralling them back under her. She let out a commanding huff, and the cubs jumped up under her scaly belly, their needle-like claws locked into the seams between her scales, their tails hooked over her back. The mother curled the excess of her tail around her midsection and tightened it around the cubs, then inched forward, hissing at Taren, joined by the high-pitched quartet beneath her.

She arched her back as if to pounce. Taren drew his Bushblade and with a single flick, the blade appeared, glinting in the fading stella grub light as he levelled it at her.

The creature hesitated and looked nervously into the starlit waters beside them. The cubs began to whimper until the mother gave them a reassuring purr. Taren lowered the Bushblade as he followed her gaze, then raised it again as their eyes met once more.

The creature's lips curled up into a snarl and looked intently past Taren to the far shore, then it took a step back and lowered its head.

"Alright," said Taren, lowering the Bushblade. "You want to get your cubs across the bridge, and so do I. Let's see if we can both get what we want."

The creature huffed.

"Alright then…" said Taren suspiciously, wondering if the creature actually understood what he said.

"Let's start, shall we?"

 Taren backed along the narrow waterbridge. His progress slowed from dividing his attention between the creature behind and the narrow path ahead. It tried to nudge closer to Taren each time he looked back but retreated each time Taren raised the Bushblade over his head.

They finally reached the other shore, and Taren quickly stepped aside. He looked for somewhere to hide out of reach but only saw sheer walls on either side. He knew if the creature wanted to kill him, his Bushblade would be no match for those scales and claws. His only hope was the beast was more interested in leaving with its cubs than eating him.

He took a deep breath and stood his ground, remembering what Arlorn had taught him. "Never run from a beast. Face them and show no fear, for if it is your time to die, nothing can prevent that, but if it's not your time… what a tale you will tell."

The creature slowly stepped off the waterbridge and leered at Taren. Its scaly heckles rose as it arched its back, its ears flattening as it prepared to strike. Taren shakily clasped his Bushblade in both hands and held his breath, trying to drown the fear that rose from his stomach.

The creature stopped, and one of its ears lifted and swivelled backwards, twitching to a sound beyond Taren's hearing. For a moment, Taren saw fear behind those eyes. The fear faded as it roared at Taren, saliva drooling from its long black fangs.

Taren raised his Bushblade higher and prepared for the end.

With a hiss, she leapt away. Her movement was so quick, Taren lost her in the shadows. He spotted her again further up the cave, silhouetted by the dung-tar lanterns. Her green eyes flashed in the silhouetted light. She unwrapped her tail from around her waist and with a shake, loosened the cubs to the ground. Then, with a flick of her tail and a nod, she gestured to her back.

One by one, the cubs hunched down and, like coiled springs, leapt onto their mother's back. All except for the littlest one who could not grip onto her smooth upper body. After several attempts, it gave up and circled her legs, whimpering at its siblings who mewed supportively from her back but still taking the time to hiss at Taren on completing each circuit of her legs.

The mother finally lost patience and swept the cub onto her back then growled at it inches from its face. The cub lowered its head, unable to meet its mother's gaze. Her disapproval was interrupted as her ears pricked up, and she stared in Taren's direction. She huffed, then with a flash of grey, vanished from sight, leaving Taren alone in the cave with the darkness approaching behind him over the water as stella grubs continued to wink out, one by one.

With a sigh, Taren re-sheathed his Bushblade. He could see the darkness coming up from behind, but a few more minutes wouldn't matter. The worst was over, and it would give the mother and her cubs plenty of time to get to wherever it was going. The last thing he wanted was to bump into it further up the cave.

One thing is sure, thought Taren to himself as he straightened his cloak. *This day couldn't get any worse.*

He was about to leave when he felt something at his feet.

He looked down and saw water from the lake silently wash over his boots. Taren slowly turned around and came face to face with his worst fear. An eight-legged crustacean, a cross between a spider and a crab, rose from the waters, three times Taren's height and as black as the lake it rose from.

Unlike a crab, it had no claws, but its hard-shelled legs were covered with clumps of fine black hairs that glistened in the fading stella grub light. Several sets of eyes on telescopic stalks glared down at him. Taren, unsure which set to look at, was mesmerised as they bobbed and weaved independently of each other. It opened its elongated mouth flanked by beckoning mandibles. Maxilla with teeth up each side like combs dripped with undigested goo. Taren clamped his hand over his mouth as his stomach surged within him from the smell.

He tried to back away, but fifteen-foot antennae had already curled down behind him and pressed into his back. Tongues slithered from the ends of the antennae; one wrapped around his neck while the other wrapped around his middle. Taren managed to unsheathe his Bushblade but was unable to open it as the tongues clamped his arms to his side and his Bushblade to his hip.

Taren struggled as the antennae lifted him from the ground, but the more he struggled, the tighter they got. He tried to scream, but no sound came out. His breath shortened, and his vision narrowed. The smell of death from the mandibles filled his nostrils as the antennae lifted him closer to his end. He shut his eyes, hoping it would be quick.

His thoughts turned to his life before Arlorn. To the orphanage and the mute girl he befriended there, and the image that haunted him every night; the fire that ended her life. The fire he was inadvertently responsible for.

He deserved this, and somewhere deep inside, he welcomed it. Finally, he would have rest from the guilt that gnawed at his very being. Taren relaxed and let himself go.

He felt darkness around him, warm and comforting, not what he expected, but it was better than what he hoped for.

As the mandibles opened to welcome him to his end, Taren heard a still small voice, then saw a sliver of light in the darkness. The voice seemed familiar somehow, and it knew his name. It breathed a word in his mind, the word taking form until a thought appeared in his head.

He had to live.

He opened his eyes and, ignoring the smell from the drooling maxilla's that made his stomach wretch, he flicked his Bushblade towards his chest. The blade opened with a jolt and cut through the antennae-tongue. Taren felt the sting of the blade as it nicked his chest, only the clasp of his cloak preventing it from burying deep into his skin. He didn't care; he was free, but he didn't get time to enjoy his freedom. The antennae-tongue around his neck tightened as it took all his weight.

Taren frantically reached for the antennae that hung like a noose above his neck, but in his panic, he dropped his Bushblade, the weapon clattering on the stony ground below. He held onto the antennae, trying to pull himself up to loosen its hold on his neck, but he was too weak. Fortunately, the antennae were unable to support Taren's weight on their own, and Taren descended to the ground, the noose loosening just enough for him to gasp a few breaths.

Taren was unable to enjoy his brief moment of respite, for the antennae had enough spring in it to lift him off the ground, if only for a moment. For the next few minutes, Taren bounced like a marionette on an elastic band, springing between heaven and earth. He used his feet to fight off the mandibles and maxilla that grasped at him on his ascent and reached desperately for the Bushblade on his descent, the antennae pulling him away as it came within reach.

As Taren ascended for the seventh time, he let go of the

antennae to fend off a ferocious attack from the mandibles and unwittingly grasped a pair of the crustacean's eyes. There was a pop, and the eyes separated from the stalks on Taren's descent. The crustacean backed away with a gargled roar. Taren hit the cold stone floor with a bump and felt something in his hand. The hilt of his Bushblade.

The crustacean lifted Taren off the ground once more, its mouth frothing as its mandibles beckoned to him. Taren swung at it with his Bushblade, severing part of the mandibles. Green goo dripped from the wound. The crustacean lowered its head, trying to protect its remaining limbs from Taren's flaying swings.

Taren reached up and severed the antennae noose above his head. A chilling scream filled the cave as Taren fell heavily to the cavern floor. He removed the remains of the tongue, gasping for breath as he rose to his feet and rubbed his aching neck.

The crustacean let out a burbled hiss and lunged at Taren, but another swing from Taren's Bushblade made it retreat. As it did, it slipped, its legs folding beneath it.

Taren saw his chance and raised his Bushblade over his head to strike the crustacean. The crustacean cowered beneath its severed mandibles, its remaining sets of eyes staring wide-eyed at the blade.

Taren tensed as he prepared to strike. The crustacean retreated further behind its mandibles. Taren paused. His face lost all expression as his blade hovered above the creature's head.

He slowly lowered the blade. The crustacean watched it nervously until it hung at Taren's side, then all of its eyes focused on Taren.

After all the crustacean had done to him, he couldn't bring himself to kill it. The crustacean only saw Taren as a meal. It had no malicious intent. It was what it was, and Taren couldn't deny that. Maybe what Arlorn told him was right. "Nothing in the swamp hates you, but be smarter than the things that want to eat you. They won't kill you without a reason, so why not do the same for them?"

Taren raised his Bushblade and stepped forward. Then spread his arms out to his side as if shooing the creature away, stomping his foot and going "He-ah... He-ah..." with each step.

The crustacean slowly rose to its feet and cautiously retreated into the waters. Its eyes fixed firmly on Taren's Bushblade until, with a 'bloop,' the last pair of eyes vanished from sight.

Taren looked out across the waters, following the ripple left by the submerged crustacean. The darkness was almost upon him. The stella grubs were already winking out where the crustacean had descended. Soon he would be left in darkness. He had to reach the lamps before the dark overtook him. There was no knowing what else could be lurking in the dark.

He shakily struggled his way along the tunnel. The thought of how close he came to death was finally sinking in, so it was a relief when he reached the lanterns. He followed the lights to the entrance. The feel of the sun on his face washed the darkness away. He closed his eyes, and he bathed in it, drawing it in as he took a moment to rest.

When he opened his eyes, he was surprised to see the mother with her cubs on her back, standing on the water's edge staring at him. He didn't have the strength for another confrontation but raised his Bushblade anyway.

With a huff, the mother turned and slipped elegantly into the water. She uncoiled her tail from the cubs, and with long strokes, glided through the waters. The littlest cub Taren had seen earlier narrowed its eyes and gave Taren a farewell hiss, making Taren smile. The cub tilted its head, and for the briefest moment, Taren thought it smiled; or maybe it was its lips curling up in a snarl as it bore its needle-like, black teeth.

The mother reached the nearest badong tree and wrapped its tail around the cubs once more. Then, with its powerful claws, she climbed onto the smooth-sided trunk. She hunched down and let out a guttural grunt, and the cubs wrapped their tails tighter around her. Then, with one bound, she jumped the length of the trunk to the canopy above, disappearing into a flurry of leaves.

A chorus of howls and hoots erupted from the canopy as birds and arboreal wildlife fled from her as she bounded effortlessly along the canopy, appearing intermittently as she jumped from tree to tree.

Taren sat by the water's edge and watched the world drift by. The occasional ripple from dark shadows broke the surface. He closed his eyes and felt the sun on his face and heard the fluttering leaves in the gentle breeze. Despite the swamp's treacherous reputation, there was a serenity to its symmetry. And for a moment, Taren felt as if he belonged.

He knew he had to return to Lorn and Arlon. He missed his bed, and Arlon was the only family he had since… He sighed, picked himself up, and straddled his Waterhog.

He smiled, for he knew he would return when he had the chance. He had his Waterhog and somewhere to stay. It would be his secret. No one else could reach this far into the swamp, and one day he would make it his home.

But for now, he would secure the Nest and stay another night. The sun shadow was already in the east, and he needed to rest his aching body. He kick-started the Waterhog, and with a roar, it came to life. He blipped the throttle and checked the gauges as the engine warmed up.

He gave the cave one last look and said a silent farewell to Fēómin. Then, with the engine roaring, he headed back to the Nest, the sound fading as he disappeared from sight.

A.J.N. Gallagher

Epilogue

In the stillness, giant insects and colourful birds flittered about. A gentle breeze fluttered through the trees, tickling ghost lichen that hung from the canopy, swaying in the ebb and flow of the gentle breeze. A weelix appeared from beneath the canopy's foliage and preened itself in the afternoon sun. It looked up. Its nose twitched nervously as its eyes darted here and there for some unseen threat, then with a howl, it scurried into the relative safety of the canopy.

Eyes appeared where the weelix had been moments before. A shimmering outline appeared around the eyes and formed into the slender form of a Skāpārī tribesman. Its body was see-through, showing the tree behind it like through glass. He sat astride a long-necked waterwalker, a hairy, bird-like creature with three eyes and three powerful legs. The middle, more powerful leg gripped the side of the trunk by its webbed and talon-tipped foot. Its ankle was contorted to hold its body and rider level, while the other two legs tucked safely up under its flightless wings.

Another Skāpārī rider appeared on the opposite side of the trunk, mirroring its counterpart. Without saying a word, they spoke to each other in mind song, only their eyes revealing the intent behind their thoughts. With a nod, they concluded their discussion. A hint of a smile appeared momentarily on their stony faces. With a tug of the reins, their beasts descended to the water, their webbed feet forming a pocket of air as they moved out onto the water's surface.

With a flick of the reins, the waterwalkers bolted, galloping with the speed of a Waterhog out into the swamp. The central leg drove them forward while the outside legs kept it stable, allowing them to weave between the trees with the grace and agility of a dancer. The riders spurred them on, rider and beast shimmering before they all vanished from sight, water rings the only sign of their passing. They were in a hurry to return to their village, for they had news, news they'd waited centuries to see fulfilled; that light had once more returned to the *Unchunee*, and with it, the prophecy that was foretold would come, had begun—on a world relegated to myth by the rest of the universe; a world known only as Génārō.

A look Inside the Nest

Language Pronunciation

A

á as in hat

ã as in ah, arm, father

â as in fare, fairy

ä as in all, call, ball

ā as in hay

E

ē as in eat

é as in met, second

ë as in tame, game

ê as in her

ę is silent

I

ī as in fine, wine

ï as in plentiful

ì as in him, in

î as in machine

O

ō as in alone, protect

ô as in nor, oar

õ as in on, off

ö as in son

ò as in too

U

ū as in tune

ú as in us

ü as in turner

Y

ÿ as in typical

y as in lyre

Génãrō is pronounced, Gén - ã(r) - ō

The 'R' is almost silent.

Emphasis is placed on the 'Gen' and the 'ō'

About the Author

A.J.N. Gallagher was born in New Zealand, where he currently resides.

Inspired by Star Wars in the seventies and living near an estuary, the first ideas for his current work in progress, Génãrõ, began to form early in his impressionable young mind and have grown ever since.

In 1990, he won a short story competition on a hunting trip with a group of others in the backblocks of Queenstown. The story was subsequently published in the N.Z. Wildlife magazine.

Allan has worked in a sushi bar, fruit orchards, and a fish and chips takeaway. He spent six months in the conservation corps. He has also sold car parts and accessories, driven tractors and trucks for silage and baleage, been a car groomer, learned joinery and wood turning.

In his spare time, he loves playing the piano. He achieved grade eight through the Trinity College of London, has a diploma in sound engineering, and was awarded a special commendation on his second year. He has recorded demo albums for others, as well as a few of his own unpublished compositions.

Archery became one of his long-time hobbies after researching archery for one of his characters. He doesn't shoot as much as he used to but achieved his twelve hundred pin in a FITA competition during that time.

His current daytime job is production manager for an electronics company specialising in telemetry-based, fail-safe devices for Effluent monitoring.

Lost in the Swamp is a novelette from the world of Génãrõ and is set five years before the main books, which are still in development.

For more information on A.J.N. Gallagher or the progress of his books, go to AJNGallagher.com

Acknowledgements

I would like to thank my Lord and Saviour, without whom I would not be here today. True to His word, He never gave up on me. It is the little things that help you get through the big stuff. And so it is with the people He sent to guide and encourage me along the way.

I would like to thank Andrew Stone, whose sermon on revisiting forgotten or discarded dreams inspired me. Without his words, I would not have picked up the baton of writing after throwing it away twenty-five years ago.

"Pick up the dreams that you thought were dead and the desires you thought were gone. They aren't gone and will spring to life like the stirring of a fire. The lightest breeze on the dullest embers can ignite a raging fire."

To my parents. Thank you for your support. I felt like I could do anything when I looked into your faces. Thank you for teaching me that "can't" has no place in my vocabulary.

Thank you to Sandi James, my long-time critique partner and dearest friend. I am in your debt, and life would be most unsavoury without you in it. I look forward to our future together.

Thank you to the L.A.B., the critique coaching group I am part of with Logan Tiberi-Warner and Brenda Rech. And for its beginnings as part of the Small Group Coaching group at DIY MFA with Jeanette Smith, our coach during the course. The diversity of the writers meshed perfectly. Thank you, Jeanette, for bringing us together.

Thank you to Word Wizards critique group, especially Aaron Betts, Richelle Aschenbrenner, and Chris Barbosa. Thank you for letting me join and allowing me to be part of a fantastic quiver of writers. As with the L.A.B., I learned so much from your insight, critique, and ideas. We are better in a group than on our own.

Thank you to Amy Ayres and again to Chris Barbosa, who were the first critique partners to read my work. The advice they gave me took me from where it was to where it was now. You were both right.

A special thank you to Gabriela Pereira, DIY MFA, and the HUB. Thank you for the courses, critiques, and Q&A sessions. I wouldn't be where I am today without you and your team's input and support into my work and without looking at other's amazing works. You got me where I needed to be and in a way that I could understand. The course and those involved were such an inspiration. I'm so proud of being a Word Nerd.

Thank you to Elana Bai for the amazing book cover and artwork. I hope to acquire your talent in the future for my other works. Your desire to realise my vision and your dedication to detail are so refreshing. Nothing was ever a problem, and you always went above and beyond to achieve the goal. I was blown away by how, with such little prompting and direction, you could come up with so much detail.

I would like to thank my editor, Jeanette Smith (jeanettethewriter.com) for her attention to detail. Not only was she my editor but also my coach in the DIY MFA Small Group Coaching course. Her motivation and insight saw the way through obstacles and helped keep me on track.

Finally, I would like to thank Linda and Murray Allison. Linda for her encouragement, especially the words. Now, more than ever, we need writers who will change people's lives. I hope I do. And thank you to Murray, her husband, for Beta reading my work. You are such an avid reader, and your insight was invaluable.

Map of Génārō